Disney
Henry HuggleMonster

Fang-tastic!

Adapted by Andrea Posner-Sanchez
from the script "Fangs Out" by Michael Stern

Illustrated by Fabio Laguna and James Gallego

A GOLDEN BOOK • NEW YORK

randomhousekids.com
ISBN 978-0-7364-3348-8 (trade) — ISBN 978-0-7364-3349-5 (ebook)
Printed in the United States of America
10 9 8 7 6 5 4 3 2 1

Henry Hugglemonster loves mornings! He turns off his roaring alarm clock, does some monster stretches, and then stomps off to start a brand-new day.

"It's really important for monsters to have a good wake-up routine," Henry tells his monster dog, Beckett. "I start by washing up."

Henry closes his eyes and covers his face with soap suds. But when he reaches for his towel, he grabs Beckett by mistake!

"Now comes the part I like best," says Henry. "Brushing my fangs!"

Henry squeezes some fangpaste onto his fangbrush and starts brushing. But something feels different. He puts the fangbrush down and wiggles one of his fangs. It's loose!

Henry runs downstairs to tell his parents the good news. Momma tells Henry about the Fang Monster. "She flies into your room at night, takes your baby fang from under your pillow, and leaves you a special gift."

"A special gift? Roar-some!" roars Henry. He wants his fang to fall out right away.

Henry's mother has an idea. She pours super-sticky monster molasses over his monstercakes. After just one bite, Henry's loose fang pops out.

"It worked!" shouts Henry. "And it didn't even hurt!"

"Way to go, kiddo!" says Daddo.

Henry is so happy, he wants to ROAR! But all that comes out is a little whistle. He tries again and the same thing happens. When Henry lost his fang, he also lost his roar!

"Oh, no!" Henry cries. "My roar is my best thing. It's what makes me Henry Hugglemonster."

Daddo explains to Henry that monster fangs grow back quickly. "Before you know it, you'll have your roar back— and a brand-new big monster fang."

Henry is sad. He leaves the kitchen and runs into his sister in the hallway. "You're just the monster I was looking for," Summer says. "I have your costume right here." She reminds Henry that he is supposed to play the Roaring Lion in her new play. "You're perfect for this part!"

Without his roar, Henry doesn't feel perfect at all.

Summer puts the costume on her brother so they can practice their big duet. *"He's the king of the jungle, royal to the core. But the coolest thing of all is his great big lion roar!"* sings Summer. But as Henry opens his mouth to roar, the doorbell rings. He slips out of the costume and rushes off to see who is there.

Denzel, Gertie, and Estelle have come to invite Henry to play Huggleball with them. Henry loves Huggleball. All you have to do is catch, throw, and run. No roaring required!

"Sorry, Summer. I can't let down my friends. They need me," he tells his sister, and he heads out the door.

The four friends run to the yard and start playing. Before long, Henry scores the first goal. The monsters let out a big ROAR! But not Henry.

"You didn't do the Score Roar," Denzel says to Henry.

"When somebody scores, we all roar," Gertie reminds him.

Henry is worried his friends will laugh at his whistle. So instead, he picks up the huggleball and keeps playing.

Gertie runs to block Henry by standing between him and the goal—but nothing can stop Henry Hugglemonster! He leaps over Gertie and scores again. Henry feels great! This time he joins his friends for the Score Roar...

. . . and lets out a whistle.
   Estelle, Denzel, and Gertie
all turn to stare at Henry.

Henry is embarrassed. But his friends love the whistle!

"I've always wanted to whistle, but never could," Denzel admits.

"Can you do it again?" Gertie asks.

"Do it again! Do it again!" Estelle chants.

When Henry whistles again, Beckett runs over and does a flip! "That is so cool!" says Estelle.

"I thought you were all going to laugh at me when you found out I lost my roar," Henry admits.

"Don't be silly," Denzel tells him. "We're your best friends!"

Henry keeps whistling and Beckett keeps flipping.

Soon, Summer comes outside. "What's going on?" she asks.

Henry finally tells his sister that he lost his roar. "All I can do is this. . . ." He whistles, and Beckett flips. "I can't be the Roaring Lion in your play, but I could be a Whistling Lion."

Summer loves that idea!

Later that day, Henry's family and friends gather
to watch Summer's play. The Whistling Lion and his
flipping lion cub are a big hit!

Momma is glad to see that Henry is feeling better about losing his roar. Henry puts his arms around Gertie, Denzel, and Estelle and tells her, "That's because I've got the most *roar*-some friends in the world!"

That night, as Henry brushes his teeth, he sees a brand-new fang already growing in. "Daddo was right—monster fangs *do* grow really fast!" Then Henry lets out a big ROAR!

"My roar is back! **Wa-hoooo!**" he cheers.

After such a *roar*-some day, Henry
has a monstrously good night's sleep!